W9-CKM-281

Will I Have
a Friend?

Will I Have a Friend?

Story by Miriam Cohen · Pictures by Lillian Hoban

Aladdin Paperbacks

Aladdin Paperbacks
An imprint of Simon & Schuster
Children's Publishing Division
1230 Avenue of the Americas
New York, NY 10020
First Aladdin Paperbacks edition, 1986
Second Aladdin Paperbacks edition, 1989
Printed in Hong Kong
Also available in a hardcover edition from
Simon & Schuster Books for Young Readers

15   14   13   12   11   10

Library of Congress Cataloging-in-Publication Data
Cohen, Miriam.
Will I have a friend?/story by Miriam Cohen; pictures by
Lillian Hoban.—2nd Aladdin Books ed.   p.   cm.
Summary: Jim's anxieties on his first day of school are happily
forgotten when he makes a new friend.
ISBN 0-689-71333-9
[1. Schools—Fiction.   2. Friendship—Fiction.]   I. Hoban,
Lillian, ill.   II. Title.
[PZ7.C6628   Wi   1989]
[E]—dc19   89-31340   CIP   AC

To Monroe, Adam, Gabriel, and Jem

When Pa was taking Jim to school for the first time,
Jim said, "Will I have a friend at school?"
"I think you will," said Pa. And Pa smiled down at him.

In the big schoolroom Pa said, "Good-bye."
Jim didn't say anything. He didn't want to say good-bye.
"Come, Jim," the teacher said.

All the boys were making noise.
All the girls were laughing.
Where was his friend?

The teacher said, "Here is Bill.
He is a rocket man." Bill said, "Rrrrrrrr,"
and he rocketed off.

Anna-Maria walked by.
She was pulling a wagon filled with blocks.
Jim looked at them. Anna-Maria skipped away.

Jim went over to a big table.

There were lumps and humps of gray clay on it.

The children were pulling and pinching, poking and patting the clay.

They were making snakes, hills, holes, and a banana.
Jim reached out and touched the clay.
It was cool and wet. When he picked it up, it was heavy.

Jim made a man.
But he did not know any friend to show him to.

Now it was orange juice and cookie time.
George said, "I want to pass the cookies!"
"Look!" shouted Bill. "I bit the moon!"
"So did I," said Anna-Maria.

Jim thought of something to say. He said it to Joseph.
But Joseph's mouth was full of cookies. He didn't answer.
The pitcher was empty. Juice time was over.

Sara was telling Margaret a secret.
Jim looked at them.
Where was his friend?

Danny was shouting, "Let's do funny tummies!"
Danny poked out his tummy and bumped Willy's.
Willy bumped Sammy's.

When they bumped they laughed and yelled,
"Hello, Mr. Funny Tummy!"
And Jim laughed, too.

The teacher called, "Come to story time!"
All the children came running.
Jim sat next to Paul.
The teacher read them a book about a monkey.

Danny jumped up. "I'm a monkey!" he said.
He put his tongue in his lip,
and stuck his fingers in his ears.
Jim thought he looked just like a monkey.

The teacher said, "It's time for monkeys to rest."
They lay down on their mats.
It was hard for them to lie still.

Jim looked at the ceiling. He scratched his foot.
Then he rolled over. Then he rolled back.
Someone was looking at him. It was Paul.
He had something in his hand.

When rest time was over, everyone got up.
"Look what I have," said Paul.
He showed Jim a tiny truck.

Jim reached out and Paul put it in his hand.

"The doors really work," said Paul.

"I have a gas pump," said Jim. "I'll bring it tomorrow."

Anna-Maria called, "Jim and Paul!
Don't you want to play?"
"OK, Jim?" asked Paul.
"OK!" said Jim.

After school, skipping home,
Jim said to Pa, "Do you know what?
I have a friend at school."
"I thought you would," said Pa.
And Pa smiled down at him.